THE MYSTERY OF
THE SOCCER SNITCH

created by
GERTRUDE CHANDLER WARNER

ALBERT WHITMAN & Company
Chicago, Illinois

Library of Congress Cataloging-in-Publication Data

Warner, Gertrude Chandler, 1890-1979.
The mystery of the soccer snitch / created by Gertrude Chandler Warner ;
interior illustrations by Anthony VanArsdale.
pages cm. — (The Boxcar children mysteries ; 136)
Summary: "A talented young soccer player in Greenfield is given the honor of
being a child mascot at an international soccer tournament in Brazil, but when an
anonymous letter insists that she doesn't deserve to go, the Aldens investigate"—
Provided by publisher.
[1. Mystery and detective stories. 2. Soccer—Fiction. 3. Gargoyles—Fiction. 4.
Brothers and sisters—Fiction. 5. Orphans—Fiction.]
I. VanArsdale, Anthony, illustrator. II. Title.
PZ7.W244 2014
[Fic]—dc23
2014002199

10 9 8 7 6 5 4 3 2 1 LB 18 17 16 15 14

Cover art by Logan Kline.
Interior illustrations by Anthony VanArsdale.

For more information about Albert Whitman & Company,
visit our web site at www.albertwhitman.com.

Contents

THE MYSTERY OF
THE SOCCER SNITCH

CHAPTER 1

The Big Day Arrives

"Benny, come on! Hurry!" called Jessie. "The soccer fest starts soon!"

Twelve-year old Jessie was wearing red, her team color.

Benny, who was six and wearing blue, trotted down the stairs. "Will there be lots of food at the soccer feast?"

"Not a soccer *feast*, silly" said Jessie. "A soccer fest!"

"'Fest' means 'festival,'" said Henry, the oldest. "I looked it up." Henry was fourteen

and was always looking things up in the dictionary on his new tablet.

"Shouldn't there be food at a festival, then?" Benny asked. "I think there should at least be peanuts and hot dogs and lemonade."

"We had breakfast a half hour ago!" Jessie said. "You ate all those pancakes! You can't be hungry yet."

"I'm not hungry yet," Benny said. "I just think there should be food!"

"The winners get coupons for a free cone at Igloo Ice Cream," Jessie said.

"I sure hope my team wins!" Benny shouted. He didn't see Jessie and Henry exchange smiles. What Jessie and Henry knew—but Benny didn't—was that *all* the children who participated would get a free cone at Igloo Ice Cream.

"Warm ups start soon," Henry said. "We should go."

"This is going to be fun!" Benny said.

"It sure will," Henry said. He was wearing the yellow and black of a referee. All week he'd been studying the referee's manual

Coach Olson had given him. The older boys and girls were assistant coaches and referees.

"Does everyone have their cleats and shin guards?" Henry asked.

"I packed everyone's equipment and an extra ball in this bag," Jessie said. She always brought extra equipment just in case someone needed it.

"Yay!" shouted Benny. "Let's go! Coach Olson said we are all marching in a big parade before the games, just like at the big tournament in Brazil!"

"At the real tournament it's called the opening ceremony," said Henry. "I think in Brazil there will be fireworks."

"I wish we could go to the big tournament!" said Benny. "Kayla is so lucky!"

A few weeks earlier, the town of Greenfield erupted with excitement when the newspaper ran a front-page story with the headline, "Greenfield Girl Chosen as International Child Mascot!" Kayla's parents and Coach Olson quickly organized a soccer fest so everyone could get into the spirit of the

upcoming international tournament. The soccer fest would last one day—an opening parade followed by a series of games, ending with an award ceremony—but the children had been practicing for the games almost each day for the past two weeks.

Now, finally, the big day was here.

"We're going to go warm up now, Grandfather!" Jessie called out.

Mr. Alden opened the door to his study. "I'll be along shortly," he said, "before the opening parade."

When Benny opened the front door, Watch, their dog, ran in from the kitchen. Watch panted excitedly, his toenails clipping across the floor.

"Don't worry, Watch," Grandfather told the dog, patting his head. "I'll bring you, too. But you can't go now. The children will be warming up."

After everyone said goodbye, Benny bounded out the door and down the steps to the street. The other three followed.

Together the children walked past

clapboard houses with neat picket fences in front and carefully tended gardens. The sky was clear blue. The air smelled of freshly cut grass and flowers. It was the perfect day for a soccer fest.

Violet felt at ease, walking like this with her brothers and sister. Although they had lost their parents, they had each other, and now, of course, they had Grandfather and Watch.

After their parents died, they ran away because they were afraid of being placed in different homes. They had lived in a boxcar in the woods and entirely took care of themselves—until Grandfather found them, and they learned he was a wonderful person. With him, they could all be together.

Violet was wearing a purple jersey, purple shorts, and lavender socks. She was shy and didn't often raise her hand to speak, but when Coach Olson asked the group of ten-year-old girls what team color they wanted, Violet raised her hand and said purple. Each team also selected the name of a professional

team. Violet's team decided to be the purple Wizards.

Getting into the spirit that morning, Violet even laced her cleats with purple shoelaces and tied her pigtails with purple ribbons.

Violet thought about the soccer fest, and parade—and Kayla Thompson. "I wonder if Kayla is excited about being a child mascot in Brazil," she said.

"Kayla has to be excited!" cried Benny. "Why wouldn't she be? Isn't that the whole reason we're having a soccer fest?"

"I don't think she's excited," Violet said. "She doesn't act excited. I understand why. She'll have to go out on the soccer field in front of millions of people."

"I don't think she's shy," Henry said. "She seems very comfortable playing soccer with lots of people watching her."

"That's true," Jessie said. "I think Kayla is just not the type to act excited."

Jessie started to say something more about Kayla, but stopped. She had a vague feeling that Kayla wasn't a very nice person. Other

girls in town openly disliked Kayla and even talked badly about her. But, Kayla's family had only recently moved to Greenfield. So nobody really knew Kayla very well. In fact, one girl, Danielle, who was clearly jealous of all the attention Kayla was getting, said Kayla wasn't really a Greenfield girl because she had only lived in the town for six months.

The Alden children arrived at the field to find it decorated with balloons and streamers. The field was large enough for three games to be played at once. Across the street by the playground was another field, also decorated. The streamers—mostly red, white and blue flapped in the breeze. Each team had a banner with their team color, team name, and the name of each player.

"There's my team!" Benny shouted. "The Earthquakes!"

The players gathered with their teams to the side of the field and did warm-up exercises. First they practiced dribbling, then they practiced passing the ball to each other.

Toward the end of their warm-up exercises,

the bleachers filled with spectators. Jessie looked over and saw Grandfather taking a seat in the bleachers. Next to him was Mrs. McGregor, his housekeeper, and several of his friends. Watch lay on the ground nearby, panting because of the heat. This time of year—late August, just after school started— always seemed like the hottest time of year.

Coach Olson blew his whistle and the teams ran to the side of the field. The high school marching band was already in formation.

Benny was jumping with excitement. All around him, small children were jumping and wiggling and good-naturedly pushing each other, eager to get started.

Jessie, watching him, smiled. Her team, all dressed in red, had chosen the name Chicago Fire.

Coach Olson blew his whistle, and the marching band marched onto the field. The drums rolled, *rat-a-tat-tat, rat-a-tat-tat*. The crowd cheered and clapped and stamped their feet. The band played "My Country 'Tis of Thee," a song Jessie always found stirring.

Next came the high school majorettes in their sequined uniforms twirling and tossing their batons. The batons glittered in the sun.

The first team to march onto the field was Jessie's team, the Chicago Fire. Leading the team was Kayla, dribbling a ball and performing fancy footwork. She did a fake, pretending she was going to pass the ball and instead stepping on it and pushing it behind her. Next she kicked the ball, causing it to fly straight up, then she bounced it twice on her shoulders. She stepped back and the ball landed directly at her feet and she began dribbling again.

I wish I could do that, Jessie thought.

The audience, many of whom had never seen Kayla's skills, shouted "oooh!" and "aaah!"

"She's just a show-off," said Danielle, one of Jessie's teammates who made no secret of her dislike for Kayla.

"Shh," whispered Jessie.

After the teams circled the field, the marching band played "Yankee Doodle

Dandy." When the last of the drums quieted, Coach Olson walked up to a small wooden platform.

He picked up his microphone. He turned it on, and it made a brief screeching sound. He cleared his throat and said, "Welcome! Welcome to the first Greenfield Soccer Fest!" His voice boomed across the field.

Everyone cheered. Jessie looked over at Grandfather and smiled. He smiled back.

"The players have been working hard," said the coach, "practicing and preparing, getting ready for today's grand tournament. Each team will play three games—"

"Stop everything!" came a shout. Mrs. Thompson, Kayla's mother, was marching angrily toward the field, holding her cell phone. "Stop everything right now!"

Everyone fell silent. Jessie could see right away that Mrs. Thompson was angry. Her face was red, her frown deep.

"What is going on?" Coach Olson asked.

Mrs. Thompson marched to the foot of the platform. "Somebody in this town has

written a letter to the mascot committee! A letter filled with horrible lies about Kayla. I just received a phone call from the committee. Now she might not get to be mascot!"

Coach Olson hadn't turned off the microphone, so Mrs. Thompson's voice carried over the entire field.

When Coach Olson flipped off the microphone, there was a screech of static, then more silence.

Jessie and the other girls on the red team turned to look at Kayla.

Kayla held perfectly still for a long moment, then buried her face in her hands.

CHAPTER 2

A Horrible Letter

Mrs. Thompson walked briskly across the field toward the red team. The coach jumped down from the platform and hurried to catch up to her. Upon reaching the girls, Mrs. Thompson touched Kayla's shoulder to comfort her. Mrs. Thompson didn't look at the other girls. Jessie still felt too astonished to speak, or even move.

"Who would do such a thing?" asked the coach, approaching.

"That's just it!" Mrs. Thompson said. "We

don't know! Whoever wrote the letter didn't sign it. But now the mascot committee wants Kayla investigated, just to make sure the things in the letter are not true."

Kayla whirled around and, keeping her face hidden, ran from the soccer field. She ran past her mother, down the street toward her home.

Then everyone, it seemed, started talking at once.

"I wonder what is in the letter!"

"I wonder who wrote it!"

"I wonder what will happen now!"

The coach and Mrs. Thompson stepped aside and whispered together. As they talked, Mrs. Thompson made angry gestures, hitting her fist into her palm and pointing toward the field.

Danielle, standing not far from Jessie but out of Mrs. Thompson's earshot, whispered, "I don't think Kayla deserved to be mascot anyway. The mascot should be someone nice, not someone who just shows off."

"I am so tired of listening to you talk mean

about Kayla," another girl told Danielle. "You just wish you could play as well as her."

"If I could play as well as her," said Danielle, twirling her ponytail, "I'd be nicer about it." Danielle had a long ponytail reaching to her waist. Her hair was very thick and blond and she was obviously proud of it.

"Maybe *you're* the one who wrote the letter," Jennifer said to Danielle.

"I did not," Danielle said, flipping her pony tail over her shoulder.

A few parents from the bleachers went to join Mrs. Thompson and Coach Olson. The parents and Coach Olson talked for several moments. Then Coach Olson strode back to the podium and turned on his microphone.

"We will continue the fest next Saturday!" he announced. "We will have the games then, and the award ceremony. The older players will practice on Tuesday and Wednesday after school, as usual. The younger players— the Earthquakes and Galaxies—can practice tomorrow at one o'clock. We should have this all sorted out by next Saturday."

Nobody in the stands moved. A slight breeze moved in the trees. From the distance came the barking of a dog. Otherwise, all was quiet.

Henry, Jessie, Violet, and Benny looked for each other, and huddled in a group.

"We need to figure out who wrote the letter," Henry whispered to his sisters and brother.

"Yes," Jessie said. "This isn't fair at all."

"I wonder if we can see the letter!" said Benny. "Do you think Mrs. Thompson has it?"

"She said she got a phone call from the mascot committee," Jessie said. "So the committee probably has it."

"That's too bad," said Henry. "If we could see the letter, we could examine the postmark and see how it was written."

"I wonder who did it," Jessie said. She was looking toward Danielle.

"Do you think it was Danielle?" Violet asked.

"Actually," Jessie said, "it could have been

any of the girls on the team, not just the ones who speak up and say they don't like Kayla. The problem is, I don't know anyone on the team who would make up lies."

"Lying is bad," Benny said.

"Lying in a letter to get someone in trouble is even worse," Henry said.

Violet looked over the group of girls wearing red. There were at least a dozen of them. "We've never started out with this many suspects before," she said.

All four of the Alden children stood still for a moment, thinking this over.

"Here comes Grandfather and Mrs. McGregor and Watch!" Benny said. Benny ran toward them. The others followed behind. Watch greeted each of the children with a sniff and wag of his tail. Benny petted Watch's back while Henry scratched the top of Watch's head.

Mr. Alden said, "Well, children, I suppose we should head home."

"I was hoping to win a cone from Igloo Ice Cream," Benny said.

"Maybe next week," Henry said.

They headed down the sidewalk. Mr. Alden took a handkerchief from his pocket and patted his forehead. "It's going to be a hot day today," he said.

"The forecast is calling for high temperatures all week," Mrs. McGregor said.

"What are we going to do today?" Benny asked. "We thought we'd be here all day!"

"Mr. Beck is working at the house," Mrs. McGregor said. "So I suppose we can start by seeing how he's doing." Mr. Beck was the handyman Mr. Alden hired when they needed work done on the house.

"And," Mrs. McGregor said, "it looks to me like you children have a mystery to solve."

Violet sighed deeply. "Poor Kayla. I feel so sorry for her."

"Me, too," Henry said. "I don't know which is worse, not getting to be an international child mascot, or knowing someone wrote a mean letter filled with lies."

"At least it shouldn't be too hard to prove that the letter was filled with the lies," Jessie

said. "Then Kayla can still be the mascot."

The first thing Violet noticed as they walked up the front walk to their house was the smell of saw dust. She and the others walked around to the side of the house. Mr. Beck was up on a ladder scooping leaves out of the gutter.

"What are you doing?" Benny asked.

"Routine summer stuff," Mr. Beck said. "I just replaced some rotted boards in the garage. Now I'm cleaning the gutters. Next I'll check the windows. You have to watch out with these old windows in the summer." He squinted up at the roof line. "And it looks like a few roof tiles are loose. I'd better fix those."

"Can I help you?" Benny asked. "I can climb the ladder, too!"

"Better not, Benny," said Mr. Alden. "I think Mr. Beck can manage just fine."

"All right," Benny said. "Let's go have a snack! I can solve mysteries better with a full stomach!"

CHAPTER 3

A Not-Quite-So-Horrible Letter

Henry was the first one at the breakfast table the next morning. While waiting for the others, he'd opened the newspaper. Ordinarily Henry read the news on his tablet, but the local Greenfield newspaper had not gone digital yet. Grandfather was happy about that. He said he liked a real newspaper over breakfast and before bed.

"Would you all come look at this?" Henry called. "Amazing!"

Jessie and Violet came running from the

kitchen. "What?" Jessie asked.

"Here's a copy of the letter to the Mascot Committee! It says here that the letter was written in the library computer lab. A reporter found a copy in the automatic save file and printed it here!"

"What does the letter say?" Violet asked.

Henry, Violet, and Jessie leaned over the table and read:

Dear Members of the Mascot Committee,

This letter is to tell you all the reasons Kayla Thompson should not be an international mascot. The mascot should be someone who is a team player and who gives soccer a good name. Kayla is not a team player. She hogs the ball. She laughs when other people make mistakes. She shows off. She is not friendly and people don't like her. For all these reasons, she should not be a child mascot.

Yours sincerely,

Concerned citizens of Greenfield, Connecticut.

All three children finished reading at the same time. They lifted their heads and looked at each other.

"But," Henry said, "some of those things aren't lies."

"Most of these things aren't lies," Jessie said, "Everything here is sort of true."

"But wait," Violet said, "isn't some of that a matter of opinion? Different people can have different opinions about whether she's friendly."

"The fact is," Jessie said, "she's not a team player. She does hog the ball."

"Does she laugh when people make mistakes?" Henry asked.

"I've never seen her laugh," Jessie said. "She's usually concentrating on what she's doing, not paying much attention to anyone else."

Just then, Benny came bounding down the stairs. "What were you hollering about, Henry?"

Before Henry could answer, Grandfather came in from his study and Mrs. McGregor brought a pitcher of fresh milk and a plate of French toast.

"My favorite!" Benny said. "French toast! With syrup!"

"I was just coming to help with breakfast," Jessie told Mrs. McGregor, "but I got so distracted by the news about Kayla!"

"What news about Kayla?" Mrs. McGregor asked.

"How about if we all sit down and talk about the news over breakfast," Mr. Alden said.

The children, Mr. Alden, and Mrs. McGregor sat at the table. Mrs. McGregor passed around a plate of French toast. When it was Benny's turn, he carefully selected the largest piece. Then he looked up and said, "Does anyone mind?"

"Go ahead, Benny," Grandfather said with an indulgent smile.

Henry poured himself a glass of orange juice, then said, "The newspaper ran a copy of the letter someone wrote to the International Mascot Committee about Kayla."

"What did the letter say?" Benny asked.

"Here," Henry said, handing him the newspaper. "You can read it yourself."

Benny squinted at the newspaper. "But I'm

eating! Read it aloud. Please!"

"Yes, please do," Grandfather said. "Then we can all hear it."

Henry read the letter aloud. When he finished, Grandfather said, "Well, that's very interesting. What do you children think?"

"I think it sounds just like what girls like Danielle are always saying about Kayla," Jessie said. "And none of those things are really lies."

"That's why we have so many suspects," Violet told Mr. Alden. "So many girls don't like Kayla. It could have been any of them."

"You know," Henry said. "I don't think writing a letter with things that are true is something a person can get in trouble for."

"But it wasn't very nice," Violet said.

"Oh I agree with that," Henry said. "It wasn't nice. But it isn't what we thought at first. And it isn't what Mrs. Thompson said. Nobody wrote a letter with lies. They wrote a letter with the truth. That's different."

"I don't think it's fair for an anonymous letter to ruin a person's chance to do some-

thing as exciting as being an international mascot," Jessie said.

"If someone didn't like Kayla," Benny said, "she should have talked to Kayla or gotten a grown-up to help."

"Exactly," Violet said. "Writing that letter was mean. Whoever wrote it should work things out with Kayla and leave the Mascot Committee out of it."

Tap, tap, tap. Everyone looked up, startled.

"What was that?" Benny asked.

"Sounds like someone is hammering outside!" Jessie said.

"Let's go see!" Benny leapt to his feet and ran to the back door. The others followed.

Outside they found Mr. Beck on the ladder again, tapping at the wood trim around the window with his hammer.

"It's Sunday!" Mrs. McGregor exclaimed. "What on earth are you doing up there?"

"Just finishing up," he said. "It's going to be so hot this week, I wanted to get the last of the work finished up this morning."

"It's hard to believe it can get hotter than

this," Henry said, wiping his brow.

"It can," Mr. Beck said, "and according to the weather report, it will."

***

Later that day, Henry told Benny, "Get ready! It almost time for your practice!"

Benny had been playing with toy cars on the living room floor. He jumped up and ran to his room to change clothes. Henry, who helped coach the youngest children, was already ready.

"I'd come with you to watch for clues," Jessie said, "but it's so hot out there!"

Jessie and Violet were at a table in the living room. Jessie was reading a book, Violet was drawing in her sketchpad.

"No need!" Henry said. "Benny and I will watch for clues."

***

Nothing unusual happened during Benny's practice—until the very end, when the players were practicing dribbling down the field. Coach Olson was watching them, shouting out reminders to watch where they

were going and touch the ball with the insides of their shoes instead of the tips of their toes. Henry looked over and saw Mrs. Thompson approaching.

The coach saw her too. He said, "Henry, take over. It looks like I need to speak to Mrs. Thompson."

Henry wished he could move closer to Mrs. Thompson and the coach to hear what they were saying, but he had no choice. He had to keep reminding the players to watch were they were going. If they were not constantly reminded to keep their eyes up, they watched their feet instead of where they were doing, sometimes crashing into each other.

Whenever Henry had the chance to look over at Coach Olson and Mrs. Thompson, he could see she seemed angry at the coach. Coach Olson seemed to cower away from her.

After they spoke a few minutes and Mrs. Thompson left, the coach blew his whistle. "Everyone take a water break!" he shouted.

Some children ran for their water bottles. Others ran for the fountain.

"She seemed angry," Henry said to the coach.

"She is," Coach Olson said. "She thinks I didn't react quickly enough and that I am not protecting Kayla. She thinks the investigation should have taken an hour and not a week."

"I don't see how an investigation can take just one hour," Henry said.

"I don't either," Coach Olson replied.

"She's a very forceful person," Henry said.

"You can say that again," said the coach. "There is something fishy about this whole thing. I don't know what, but something doesn't seem right."

CHAPTER 4

Captain of the Team

When Jessie arrived for practice Tuesday, several of the girls, including Kayla, were already there. Kayla was dribbling down field. The other girls, as usual, were trying to get the ball away from her. The first thing Jessie noticed was that Kayla was smiling. It wasn't a big, happy smile. Kayla just wasn't the type to wear big happy smiles. But she was smiling. Her face was bright.

Then Kayla turned and passed the ball to Samantha. That was different! Kayla rarely

passed the ball to anyone. Jessie understood why Kayla rarely passed the ball. The other girls often fumbled and lost the ball. Kayla knew she could do better if she kept the ball to herself.

"Nice work, Kayla and Samantha!" shouted Mia.

Mia was the fifteen-year-old girl who was helping coach Jessie's team.

Jessie felt eager and hopeful. Perhaps everything was resolved. Why else would Kayla suddenly be behaving differently? Perhaps the letter writer stepped forward, apologized and took everything back, and the investigation was over. Perhaps, too, Kayla learned her lesson and would be nicer now when she played. Jessie hoped so.

Jessie put on her shin guards, and changed from her sneakers to her cleats. She took the extra balls from her bag and brought them to the field.

Betsy, one of Jessie's friends, ran up and said, "Hi there, Jess!" Betsy also seemed to be smiling. Nobody would have known, from

how all the girls were behaving, that a scandal recently rocked the town.

"Hi," Jessie said. "Everyone looks so happy. Is anything new?"

"Nothing is new. Kayla got here early. She's acting different. Much nicer. C'mon. Let's play!"

Betsy ran to join the girls, who were then down field taking turns kicking the ball into the goal. Jessie followed. Just then, Kayla passed the ball to another teammate so the other girl could practice scoring.

"See," Betsy said quietly to Jessie. "She's acting different. She's being more of a team player."

"She probably wants to show that the things in the letter aren't true," Jessie said.

"But everyone knows they *are* true!" Betsy said, and darted away.

Jessie followed. She was thinking people can change. Wouldn't it be nice if the letter ended up helping Kayla see her bad behavior? Jessie smiled at her own thoughts. Usually Violet was the optimistic one.

"Whew, it's hot!" Danielle called out. "I need more water!" She ran to the side of the field for her water bottle.

"Just pour the water right on your head!" advised Lara. "I did that and I feel great!"

Lara, indeed, was dripping with water. Danielle laughed and poured water on her own head. She also poured water on her long pony tail. Then several other girls, including Jessie, did the same. Jessie laughed. She felt much cooler.

After they'd been practicing a half hour, Mia said, "It's so hot, I think we should stop early."

The girls standing nearby agreed.

Jessie went to drink some more water. Some of the girls gathered to the side of the field, not far from her. That was when Jessie heard Danielle talking quietly to Ashley. "What's happening with the investigation? Did anyone find out who wrote that letter?"

"The coach is investigating. Didn't he talk to you yet?"

"No," Danielle said.

"He talked to me," Ashley said. "I think he's talking to everyone. You'll get a turn. Then you can tell him what you think of Kayla."

Jessie turned away, disappointed. She had hoped the problems had been resolved. She sighed. She supposed the coach would talk to her, too. When it was her turn, she would tell him she didn't think it fair for Kayla to get punished because of an anonymous letter.

"Gather around!" Mia called. "The coach says all the teams need to select a captain. He says we should have done that in the first place. So does anyone want to nominate someone?"

Jessie raised her hand. "I nominate Kayla. She is the best player. I like how she played today, during practice."

"All right," Mia said. "Kayla is nominated. Any other nominations?"

"I nominate Jessie," Betsy said. "Jessie is a good player, too."

Other girls nodded in agreement. Jessie was the second best player on the team.

"Any other nominations?" Mia asked.

"I nominate Danielle," Ashley said.

"Anyone else?" Mia asked.

Nobody said anything.

"Okay," Mia said. "We have three nominations. That should be good enough." She handed everyone a piece of paper and passed around pencils. "The votes will be secret. Everyone can write one name."

After everyone finished writing, Mia collected the pieces of paper. She went to sit by herself to count the votes. She came back and said, "Jessie wins. Jessie is the team captain."

The girls nearby turned to congratulate Jessie.

"Being team captain is a big responsibility," Mia said. "The team captain looks out for everyone. If you aren't sure what to do in the middle of the game, look at Jessie. She'll make the decisions."

Betsy leaned close to Jessie and whispered, "You'll be great!"

"Thanks," Jessie whispered back. She felt

flattered—and sorry for Kayla. She believed Kayla should have been team captain. After all, Kayla was the best player.

"Let's meet back here at the same time tomorrow," Mia called out. "Don't forget to bring a water bottle! Tomorrow is supposed to be even hotter." Then Mia turned to Jessie and said, "Coach Olson wants to know if Henry can help me coach your team tomorrow. Coach Olson said he's a really good coach."

"I'll ask him," Jessie said, "but I'm sure he can."

Jessie removed her shin guards and changed from her cleats to her sneakers. She was walking home when she saw Kayla, by herself, sitting on a bench by the playground, tying her shoe laces.

Jessie approached her. With a friendly smile, she said, "Hello."

Kayla glanced at Jessie. "Hello," she responded. Her eyebrows went into a high arch, and there was a surprised lilt to her voice. Obviously she wasn't used to people being friendly to her.

Jessie decided it was best just to come right out and say what nobody wanted to say. "I saw that letter in the paper. I thought it was terrible, and very unfair."

Kayla grimaced. It was almost as if a dark cloud passed over her face. Instantly Jessie regretted her words. She should have realized the whole subject would be painful for Kayla. She hadn't intended to cause Kayla more pain. She just wanted to be friendly.

"Thanks," Kayla said. She stood up and picked up her soccer bag. "I think I'll go now."

Just before leaving, Kayla said, "Thanks for nominating me. And congratulations on being elected team captain."

"It should have been you," Jessie said.

Kayla gave a sad, wistful smile, then waved and walked away.

***

At the dinner table that evening, Jessie told Henry that the coach wanted to know if he'd help coach her team. "Of course," said Henry. "Helping Mia will be fun."

"Did anything interesting happen at your practice?" Benny asked.

"Well, the team elected me captain," Jessie said.

"Congratulations!" Grandfather said. "That's an honor! It means your teammates respect you and look to you as a leader."

"I think Kayla should have been captain," Jessie said.

"The captain isn't always the best player," Henry said. "The captain is the best team player, the one who looks out for everyone else and chooses which plays the team should do."

"I will tell you this," Jessie said. "If Danielle or Ashley wrote the letter, they're clever about pretending they didn't. Danielle and Ashley talked about the letter as if they didn't write it, and didn't know who did."

"You'd think whoever wrote the letter would have known about the automatic save function at the library," Henry said.

"The what?" Benny asked.

"Kids were always losing their homework when they forgot to save their work," Henry said. "So now there is an automatic save. Don't you remember? That's how the reporter found the copy."

"So whoever wrote the letter doesn't know about the autosave?" Jessie asked. "I wonder if there are any clues in that."

"I think all the older kids know about autosave," Henry said. "And the teachers know."

"Maybe it wasn't one of the kids or teachers," Benny said. "Maybe it was a grown-up in town who doesn't like the Thompsons."

"Well, Benny," Henry said. "How about if tomorrow before Jessie's practice you and I

visit the library and see if we can find out if anyone other than teachers or students were using the computers."

"Good idea!" Benny said.

***

The next day, at school, Jessie was in the school library during her study period when she felt a gentle tap on her shoulder. She turned. There was Coach Olson, smiling.

"May I speak to you for a few minutes," he asked.

"Of course!" Jessie said.

Jessie and Coach Olson sat at the table in the library conference room. Coach Olson had an open friendly face and an easy smile.

"You probably know why I want to talk to you," he said. "I am investigating the accusations in the letter. The mascot committee wants to know whether they are true."

"You should have seen how nice Kayla was at the practice yesterday!" Jessie said. "She passed the ball to other girls so they could score, too. She was friendly, and a team player."

"But she generally isn't a team player, right? Ordinarily, she does not show team spirit. Do you agree with that?"

Jessie looked down into her lap. She understood why Mrs. Thompson was not happy with the coach, since it was clear he didn't like Kayla, and didn't think she should be mascot.

"Kayla is the best player on the team," Jessie said. "By far. I think she can learn to be a team player, if someone helps her."

The coach smiled at her and said, "You are very supportive of your teammates. All of them. Mia said that's why you were elected team captain."

Jessie felt confused, wondering why he was suddenly talking about her.

"Thank you," she said.

***

The downtown library was crowded after school. "I'll bet everyone wants to be in here where it's nice and cool," Benny whispered to Henry.

Henry agreed. All the comfortable reading

chairs were taken. The carpet in the picture book room was also filled with children sprawled out, reading. Henry and Benny walked to the back of the library where the row of computers were lined up on a table against the back wall. A few kids were doing homework. Several of the computers were empty. Benny and Henry sat down and looked around.

One of the librarians came to them and said, "Can I help you boys with anything?"

"We were curious about that letter the reporter found," Henry said.

"Very clever of that reporter," said the librarian. "She came in and asked if the computers had automatic save functions. I said they did, and she said she wanted to look for something. She spent about twenty minutes looking through one homework assignment after another. Then she found the letter."

"I only see students using the computers," Henry said. "And sometimes teachers."

"Mostly students," said the librarian. "But

occasionally we get adults, too, who are not connected to the school."

"Do you need a library card to use the computers?" Benny asked.

"Nope, anyone can use them. We charge for printing, but anyone can print."

A boy sitting at a computer nearby raised his hand for help. The librarian excused herself and went to help him.

Benny and Henry looked at each other.

"The letter was typed, so there are no clues in the handwriting," Benny said.

"And the postmark probably shows that it was mailed from the Greenfield post office. No clues there."

"I don't think we learned anything helpful," Benny said.

"I don't think so, either," Henry said with a sigh.

CHAPTER 5

Danielle Does Something Mean

Wednesday was the hottest day yet. The air was so humid that simply walking across the street was enough to make a person feel groggy, hot, and tired. Some of the teams cancelled their practice, but the red team decided to practice anyway, even though it seemed to Jessie that the heat was making everyone feel a little cross.

When Jessie and Henry approached the field, Mia called out, "I'm so glad you could come help, Henry!"

The field was freshly mowed, so the air smelled of cut grass. Ordinarily the smell of cut grass was one of Jessie's favorite smells because it reminded her of summer. But today, the smell seemed too heavy and sweet. She was so hot she felt wet all over.

It was Jessie's turn to be the goalie. She stood waiting in front of the goal while Danielle dribbled the ball toward her. Just when it looked as if Danielle would easily kick the ball into the goal, Kayla darted in front of her, as if from nowhere, and with a single kick, took the ball away from her. In a flash, Kayla was dribbling in the other direction.

"Show-off!" Danielle said, flipping her long pony tail over her shoulder.

"I'm not showing off," Kayla said. "I'm playing soccer the way you're supposed to play soccer."

"You're always showing off," Danielle said.

"You're always being mean," Kayla retorted. "You and your mean friends."

Betsy said to Danielle, "You just don't like

that Kayla can get the ball away from you so easily."

Danielle turned away, but not before Jessie saw the angry look that crossed her face. Jessie braced herself, waiting for Danielle to say something else mean. But Danielle didn't say anything. She put both hands in the pockets of her shorts. Jessie thought that was odd.

A few minutes later, Henry blew his whistle and called out to Danielle, "Why are you running with your hands in your pockets?"

Danielle ignored him. She kept her hands in her pockets.

Henry and Jessie exchanged puzzled glances. "We'd better keep an eye on them," Jessie said.

"Oh, yes," Henry said.

"Can someone else have a turn being goalie now?" Jessie asked. The goalie has to stay near the goal. Jessie wanted to stay close to Danielle and Kayla.

"Certainly," Mia said, "if you don't want to any more."

"How about Jennifer?" Jessie suggested. "She hasn't had a turn yet."

Jessie took off the goalie's vest and threw it to Jennifer. As the girls ran up and down the field, practicing, Jessie made sure to stay between Danielle and Kayla. She wanted to be able to prevent trouble, if she could. She knew from the way Kayla and Danielle looked at each other that both of them were still angry.

Ashley was dribbling toward the goal. Kayla easily stole the ball from her, then turned and dribbled the opposite direction.

Just then, in a flash, Danielle darted in front of Kayla. She took something from her pocket and dropped it on the ground at Kayla's feet.

Kayla tripped. She screamed and sprawled forward. She landed face down, in the grass.

Jessie ran to Kayla, and knelt next to her. "Kayla! Are you okay?"

Kayla pushed herself up to a sitting position. She had grass stuck to the side of her jersey and some mud on her face.

Others, including Henry, ran over and knelt next to Kayla.

"I'm fine," Kayla said. Jessie could see she was shaky and angry. Mia ran to them. Together, Jessie and Mia helped Kayla to her feet.

Kayla looked down to see what she'd tripped on. There, on the ground at her feet, was a golf ball. Kayla picked up the golf ball, and marched over to Danielle. "Did you do this?"

Jessie ran to be next to Kayla. "It's okay, Kayla," Jessie said. "Let's not have a fight."

Kayla shook the golf ball at Danielle. For a horrible moment, Jessie thought Kayla was going to throw it at her. Instead, Kayla whirled around and said, "I'm finished."

Kayla dropped the ball into her own pocket. She went to the bench, picked up her water bottle and sports bag, and walked from the field. The other girls were silent, watching, as she crossed the street and sat on a bench. She changed from her cleats into her regular shoes.

"Maybe we should stop for today," Mia said. "Everyone is a little testy."

"You can say that again!" one of the girls said.

"I'm glad she won't be mascot," Ashley said.

Jessie shot Ashley a quick glance. She couldn't understand how anyone could take sides against the girl who had just been tripped. Jessie looked closely at Ashley. Maybe Ashley and Danielle were the ones who had written that letter to sabotage Kayla's chances.

"My opinion," Mia said, "is that Jessie should be mascot."

"I don't want to be mascot," Jessie said quickly. "I wouldn't want to take something away from someone else like that."

"But you're the kind of player who *should* be mascot," Mia said.

The girls sat on benches to change into their sneakers. Jessie put her shin guards and the extra balls she had brought into her soccer bag and slung the bag over her shoulder.

Henry and Jessie walked home together. It seemed to Jessie that the entire town was moving in slow motion because of the heat. There were not many cars on the street, and only a few people on the sidewalk.

"Mrs. McGregor asked if we can stop at the market for some milk," Henry said. "That's why I brought this." He pointed to the backpack he was wearing.

"All right," Jessie said.

They turned a corner toward the market and there, in front of them, was Kayla, heading toward her house. Kayla's hands were in her pockets.

"You sure are right about those girls," Henry said. "They can be mean."

"Yes, they can," Jessie agreed. "Ever since Kayla came to the school, the girls have been mean to her."

Kayla was walking faster than Henry and Jessie, so soon she was at the corner, ready to cross the street. Idly, as Henry and Jessie watched, Kayla took the golf ball from her pocket, looked at it, and rubbed it against

her shirt the way a person might brush off an apple before eating it. Then she dropped it back into her pocket. She turned the corner and was gone from their sight.

Henry and Jessie turned the corner toward the market. Henry looked down an alley where Gerry's General Store used to be. The sign still said, "Gerry's General Store," even though Gerry had closed his store and

moved from town over the winter. There was a "For Lease" sign in the window.

"Would you look at that!" Henry said. "The window is broken!"

Jessie peered down the street. "It is!" she said. At first she hadn't noticed because the storefront was in shadows.

"I wonder when that happened," Henry said. "I didn't notice it this morning. We should tell Grandfather so he can let the police know."

"Maybe we should look," said Jessie, "to make sure nothing was left dangerous."

Henry and Jessie quickly walked down the alley to the store. Glass was everywhere. The wood casing was splintered.

Just then a door opened and Mrs. Leob, a friend of Grandfather's, came out of a nearby shop. Seeing the broken glass, she shrieked. She turned to Henry and Jessie, "Did you do this?"

"No, ma'am, we did not!" Henry said. "We saw the broken glass and came over to look."

Mrs. Leob looked closely at Henry and Jessie. "Oh! You're the Alden children! I was

so upset I didn't notice! Did you see anything suspicious?"

"No, ma'am," Henry said.

"I will call the police right away," Mrs. Leob said. "We do not put up with this sort of behavior in Greenfield. Whoever did this will find himself—or herself—in big, big trouble."

Just then, Jessie noticed something else. Cold air was coming from the inside of the store. "It seems like an air conditioner is on in there," Jessie said.

"You're right!" Henry said. "The air is freezing! How odd!"

"What a waste of energy," Mrs. Leob said. "I will have the police turn it off when they get here."

CHAPTER 6

A Friend in the Woods

Meanwhile, Violet was at home. The purple team didn't practice that day. Their coaches—two eighth-grade girls—said it was simply too hot. So Violet did her homework, then sat in the living room with her sketch pad. She was in an after school art class which met once weekly, on Mondays. Grandfather bought her a new sketchpad for the class. Already she'd filled most of her sketchpad with lovely drawings.

She pulled a chair to the window. From

the chair, she could see the flowerbeds in the front yard. She drew the rosebushes. She liked drawing nature—trees, flowers, birds. After filling a few pages with drawings of the flowerbed, she went to Grandfather's study. His door was open and he was at his writing desk, working. She tapped softly on the door frame.

He looked up.

"Grandfather, may I take my sketch book into the woods so I can draw some trees and wild flowers."

"Certainly," he said. "Take some water with you to drink. And don't forget to be back by dinner time."

She walked from the house, down the street to the trail leading into the woods. A short distance into the woods, she found a cool glade. She spread a blanket in the shade and settled down with her sketch pad and drawing pencils. There, in a sunny spot, was a patch of beautiful pink flowers with five soft petals and a yellow center. She knew the names of the flower from a book she'd

read in school the year before. The flowers were called pasture roses, but they didn't look anything like garden roses. They had a simple shape, just five petals, so they were easy to draw.

Soon she filled her sketchbook page with pasture roses. She was drawing grass to frame the picture when she heard the crunching of footsteps through the woods. The person was coming from the opposite direction Violet had come, so she suspected whoever was approaching was not her sister or one of her brothers.

She looked up and waited.

To her surprise, from around the corner, came Kayla, carrying a sketch pad. Kayla stopped, obviously surprised to see Violet. The two girls looked at each other for a moment.

Kayla said, "Sorry," and turned to leave.

"You can stay," Violet said. "This is a nice place to draw."

Kayla hesitated. Violet noticed Kayla had a serious sort of face. Her lips were thin and

a bit pale, her eyebrows were light, her eyes a cool gray-blue. She didn't seem like the kind of girl who smiled much.

Violet made room on her blanket. Kayla sat down and took out a sharpened pencil and began to sketch a nearby tree.

Violet tried not to watch. She tried to concentrate on her own picture. But Kayla was sitting close enough so Violet couldn't help but see what Kayla was drawing.

"That's really good," Violet said. Violet wasn't just being nice. Kayla's picture was good. Kayla sketched with light, soft touches of her pencil, perfectly capturing the rough texture of the bark and the shape of the trunk.

"So is yours," Kayla said.

"I like to draw," Violet said.

"Me, too," Kayla said.

Violet returned to her drawing, deeply surprised. Kayla was nothing at all like she expected. She'd had the feeling all along that people were wrong about Kayla. Now she knew for sure that people were misjudging her.

The girls sat quietly, drawing, until Violet noticed, from the slant of the sun, that dinner time was approaching.

"I should go home now," she said. "I'm supposed to be back before dinner."

"Me, too," said Kayla, standing up.

Kayla helped Violet fold up her blanket. Just before Kayla turned to go, she said, "Thank you for not saying anything about you-know-what. I am tired of talking about it."

"I understand," Violet said.

"Even when people are being nice, I don't like talking about it."

"I understand," Violet said again. And she did. Violet didn't like to talk much either, particularly to people she didn't know well.

***

When the Aldens were sitting at the dinner table, eating, Violet said, "I saw Kayla in the woods today. She seemed very nice."

"What were you doing in the woods?" Henry asked. "What was *she* doing in the woods?"

"Drawing. We were both drawing."

The Aldens were silent for several minutes. Then Henry said, "Grandfather, there was a big broken window in town on Fifth Street. The store that used to be Gerry's General Store."

"I heard about that," Mr. Alden said. "I was in town about an hour ago, getting my hair cut, when Mrs. Leob reported the broken window. The police think it was vandalism."

"What's vandalism?" Benny asked.

"That means someone broke the window on purpose," Henry said. "Why do the police think it was vandalism?"

"Because just inside the broken window, on the floor, were several golf balls."

"Golf balls!" Jessie exclaimed. She and Henry looked at each other.

"Very curious," Henry said.

"What's curious about that?" Benny asked.

Jessie told the family about what had happened at practice, how Danielle tripped Kayla with a golf ball, and how Kayla put the ball in her pocket and carried it home.

"That is funny!" Benny said. "Usually you never hear anything about golf balls! But suddenly there are golf balls everywhere!"

"There may be something about the broken window in the evening paper," Henry said. "Grandfather, may I get your newspaper?"

"Certainly," Mr. Alden said.

Mr. Alden's newspaper was still folded just inside the front door. Henry picked up the newspaper and returned to the table. He rolled off the rubber band and opened the paper. There, on the Town News page, was a short mention of the broken window, only a few sentences in length. Henry read the sentences to his family:

"The window of Gerry's General Store was found broken this afternoon. Golf balls were found on the floor, just inside. The police suspect vandalism."

"We didn't learn anything at all new from that," Jessie said.

"Except now we have another mystery to solve!" Benny said.

CHAPTER 7

The Mystery of the Golf Balls

"Did you hear?" Danielle said to Jessie the next day on the black-top.

The paved area in back of the school where the kids waited for the bell was called the black-top because the pavement was so dark. The only problem with waiting on the black-top was the asphalt heated up on hot days. It was still early, and already Jessie could feel the heat coming up from the pavement. On hot days, the black-top smelled of tar.

"Hear what?" Jessie asked.

"Kayla broke the window of the old General Store," Danielle said.

Jessie was so startled, all she could say was, "What?!"

"A golf ball was found just inside the window. Remember when Kayla left practice? She was mad. And she had a golf ball in her pocket."

"She did not break the window," Jessie said. "She couldn't have. Henry and I saw her with the golf ball after the window was already broken."

"Who else would have done it?" Danielle said. "Don't you remember how mad she was?"

"I remember," Jessie said. "She was mad because *you* tripped her!"

"She wasn't just mad at me," Danielle said to Jessie. "She was angry in general because now she doesn't get to be mascot."

"We don't know that for sure," Jessie said. "Someone wrote a letter and there is an investigation."

"I don't think she will be allowed to be

mascot," Danielle said. "I don't think Coach Olson likes Kayla very much. I don't think he likes Kayla's mother, either. She is very pushy."

"Listen," Jessie said. "Kayla couldn't have broken the window. I saw Kayla with that golf ball after the window was broken. Besides, the newspaper said several golf balls were found in the store. Kayla only had one."

Danielle shrugged. "The newspaper could have accidentally printed 'golf balls,' when they meant 'golf ball.'"

"I really doubt that," Jessie said.

Ashley was standing nearby with a group of girls. "Hey, Ashley!" Danielle called. "Don't you think Kayla was the one who broke the window?"

"You're spreading rumors!" Jessie said to Danielle.

Danielle ignored Jessie and said, "Hey, Ashley, what do you think? Kayla was the one with a golf ball, right?"

Ashley gave a quick shrug, but didn't look directly at either Jessie or Danielle. "Could

be," Ashley said. "She was awfully mad at you." Ashley turned away.

Jessie watched Ashley curiously. There was something strange about the way Ashley acted.

***

"I did *not* break that window," Kayla said adamantly when someone asked her about it during lunch. Jessie was eating her lunch with a few friends at the next table. She hadn't noticed that Kayla had been sitting not far away, eating her lunch alone.

"Who else would have done it?" the girl asked.

"I don't know!" Kayla said. Ordinarily Kayla was aloof and a bit detached. Now there was deep passion in her voice.

Jessie felt she had to do something. She excused herself from her friends, and walked to Kayla's table.

"I know Kayla didn't do it," Jessie said.

"How do you know?" asked a boy sitting nearby.

"My brother Henry and I saw Kayla walking home yesterday. She still had the golf ball in her pocket. At the same time, we

saw the window already broken. Besides, the police report said there were golf balls found inside the window. Kayla had only one."

Kayla looked at Jessie with gratitude and astonishment. The other kids were silent.

"So I know Kayla didn't do it," Jessie said quietly.

"Who do you think did it, then?" another boy sitting nearby asked Jessie.

"I don't know," Jessie said. "But not Kayla."

"Maybe," suggested one of Jessie's friends, who had come over to listen better, "whoever wrote the letter also broke the window because they want to make Kayla look bad."

"That's what my parents think," Kayla said. "They think someone did it and is blaming it on me." Kayla looked directly at Ashley and Danielle. Once again Ashley got a strange look on her face. She turned red and looked away.

Yes, there was something very odd in Ashley's behavior.

***

Jessie's gym period was the last period of the day. Ordinarily she liked having gym

class last. She played hard at sports, which meant after gym she was tired and ready for a very long rest. In a heat wave like this one, though, it meant gym class was during the hottest time of the day.

Jessie's class was playing soccer. Soccer was a fall sport, so the first unit of the school year was always soccer. Because so many people liked soccer, Coach Olson joked that playing soccer first was a good way to get everyone excited about returning to school.

Coach Olson watched the class play. He held a clipboard and made notes. After the game, he met with each girl for a few moments and gave pointers to help them improve.

When it was Jessie's turn, he said, "I'm pleased with your game. Your dribbling and ball control are particularly good. You need to work on keeping an eye on the whole field so you know where there is an open player."

Jessie understood exactly what he meant. Sometimes she was so busy watching the ball, she forgot to keep an eye on the entire field to keep track of where the players were. It was

particularly important for her to keep an eye on the entire field because she was team captain.

Then Coach Olson startled her by saying, "Jessie, I believe you are the girl who should be an international mascot. You're a true team player. You are a credit to the game. Mia thinks so, too."

"I would love to be the mascot," Jessie said. "Don't get me wrong. Going to Brazil! Watching an international tournament! It

would all be thrilling. But—" Jessie broke off and looked away. This was the hard part to explain. "I just wouldn't feel right about taking the honor away from Kayla because of an anonymous letter."

"If Kayla doesn't deserve it," the coach said, "but you do, you're not really taking anything away from her."

"I know Kayla didn't break the window. I told you. Henry and I saw her with the golf ball after the window was already broken."

"We will find out who broke the window," the coach said. "Don't worry about that. The police have ways of figuring these things out."

***

After school that day, Violet went to the glade in the woods to draw. She secretly hoped Kayla would come again.

After filling two pages of her sketchpad with drawings, she was about to give up and return home when she heard footsteps coming down the trail. Sure enough, Kayla emerged from the path carrying a sketch pad and a beach blanket.

Violet smiled. Without a word, Kayla spread her blanket near Violet and took out her drawing pencils. The girls drew in silence for a long time. At last, Violet said, "You should sign up for the after school art program. We meet on Mondays and get drawing and painting lessons."

"I would like to," Kayla said. "But I don't think my parents would like that."

"Why not?"

"This is soccer season. They want me to practice. My sister got on the high school soccer team. They want me to be able to make the high school team, too."

"But you will!" Violet said. "You're so good!"

"A good player can always get better," Kayla said. "That's what my parents say."

What startled Violet most was there was sadness in Kayla's voice.

"You don't want to practice soccer?" Violet asked.

"Not all the time," Kayla said.

"Why did you want to be a mascot?"

"I didn't. My parents filled out the application for me. I didn't even know they had done that."

The two girls went back to their drawings. After a while, Kayla said, "My parents have high hopes for me. Mom says I'm a natural. Dad says I have real talent for soccer. They think I can be the best soccer player in the family, if I apply myself."

"But you don't want to," Violet said, deeply astonished. Kayla wasn't at all the kind of person people thought she was.

"I used to think all children played soccer," Kayla said. "I used to think all families spent their weekends playing soccer or watching soccer. I was in third grade before I realized not all families are like mine."

"Most people would think you're lucky," Violet said, "to have parents who play soccer with you all the time."

"I know," Kayla said. That was all she said. Violet, who understood how it felt to be inward and shy, didn't push her to say any more.

CHAPTER 8

The Clue of the Broken Glass

Benny was at the kitchen table doing homework when Mrs. McGregor called out to Grandfather, "Would you like some iced coffee before dinner?"

"I would love some!" he responded. "Thanks!"

Benny was adding a row of numbers. He was concentrating so hard he hardly noticed the grinding of the coffeemaker, or even the sound of Mrs. McGregor whistling as she worked.

Suddenly Mrs. McGregor let out a little shriek, then exclaimed, "Oh, no!"

Benny, startled, dropped his pencil. "What's the matter?"

"Oh, fiddlesticks!" she said. "Would you look at that! The glass broke. I put ice into the coffee, and bang! The glass broke!"

"How?"

"It was silly of me. The glass was too thin, and got too hot. Then I put in the ice. Oh fiddlesticks!"

Sure enough, there on the counter, were pieces of broken glass.

"I'll help clean it up!" Benny shouted.

"No, please stay back. I don't want you to get cut. Stay here. I'll get the dustpan."

Just then the phone rang. "Stay put," Mrs. McGregor said. "Let your grandfather answer it. There might be glass on the floor. I don't want you to step on it."

Benny heard grandfather's steps in the hallway. "Hello," Grandfather said. There were a few moments of silence while Grandfather listened to whoever was talking.

Then he said: "Really? Jessie?"

"That is quite an honor," Grandfather said, "but I am not sure how Jessie will feel about it. Yes . . . yes. . .I will talk to her."

"All right, then," he said. "Goodbye." He hung up the phone.

Jessie came into the room. "Grandfather?" she asked. "What is it?"

"That was Coach Olson," Mr. Alden said. "He is still working on the investigation. He says the investigation will not be complete until the police figure out who broke the window, but meanwhile, he believes all the things in the letter about Kayla are true. He thinks the honor should go to Jessie, who he says is much nicer and more nurturing of her teammates. So what he wants to do, when the police figure out who broke the window, is suggest to the committee that Jessie should be invited to Brazil as a child mascot instead."

Jessie and Benny looked at each other.

"I told him it was an honor," Grandfather said quietly.

"Of course it's an honor!" Jessie said,

recovering from her surprise enough to speak. "Going to Brazil to see the international tournament would be amazing! But I can't possibly go! I just don't think it's fair to Kayla! This will be so humiliating for Kayla. It's wrong to give it to me instead."

"Coach Olson doesn't think so," Grandfather said. "He said the committee wants the mascot to be someone who sets a good example for the sport, not just plays well."

"It just isn't right," Jessie said.

"If that's how you feel," Grandfather said, "We can tell Coach Olson not to nominate you because you don't want to accept."

"I'll think about it," Jessie said.

***

After the children finished their homework, Jessie called a meeting so they could look at their clues.

"We have to get to the bottom of this," she said. "I will not be able to accept the invitation to be mascot as long as it looks like someone has it in for Kayla."

"People are wrong about Kayla," Violet said. "Kayla is a nice person. I know she is. People just don't understand her. I don't think she cares that much about soccer. I think she only plays because her parents want her to."

"I will tell you what I'm wondering," Henry said. "I am starting to wonder if Coach Olson is behind this. It's clear Kayla's mother and Coach Olson don't like each other much. It's also clear Coach Olson doesn't like Kayla. And Jessie is his favorite. I've heard kids say that."

"You think Coach Olson wrote the letter?" Jessie asked. "I can't believe a coach would do that. Anyway, why would he write an anonymous letter? Why wouldn't he just call the committee and say Kayla should not be mascot because she sets a bad example?"

"Maybe because he doesn't want Kayla's family any madder at him," Henry said.

"But why would Coach Olson write a letter from the library computer?" Jessie asked. "Wouldn't he know about the automatic save function?"

"Maybe he wants people to think a kid did it," Henry said.

"I just can't believe it was Coach Olson," Jessie said. "I think it was one of the girls on the red team. Maybe Ashley or Danielle or someone who is staying quiet."

"What about that broken window?" Benny said. "Probably the same person who wrote the letter also broke the window so Kayla would be blamed, right?"

"It sort of looks like that," Henry said.

"Coach Olson would never break a window," Jessie said.

"I agree with that," Henry said. "So maybe it wasn't Coach Olson after all."

"We need to figure out who broke the window!" Benny said. "Then we might have a clue who wrote the letter!"

The others nodded in agreement.

"We don't have any real clues at all about the broken window," Henry said. "Do we?"

"None," Jessie said. "Maybe fewer clues than who wrote the letter."

"What do we know about the window?"

Henry asked. "Was there anything at all unusual?"

They were all silent. "The only thing I can think of," Jessie said, "is when we went to look at the broken window, the air conditioner was blowing. I guess that means someone was inside and turned it on."

"Also it was a very old window," Henry said. "The wood was splintered and the glass was a murky color."

Suddenly Benny said, "Maybe it's like putting ice in hot coffee!"

The others looked at Benny, puzzled.

Seeing their expressions, Benny said, "Putting ice in hot coffee can break glass if the glass is too thin! Just ask Mrs. MacGregor!"

The children went to find Mrs. MacGregor, who said, "Yes, indeed. That was silly of me. The ice in the hot coffee broke the glass. I should have known that glass was too thin."

"I wonder if the same thing can happen with windows," Henry said. "Remember Beck said something about having to be careful with these old windows in the summer."

"After dinner," Jessie said, "let's go ask him."

***

After dinner all four children walked the five blocks to Mr. Beck's house. He lived in the part of town where the houses were mostly painted white, with clapboard sides and picket fences in front. The lawns and flower beds were neatly trimmed. Mr. Beck's white van was parked in his driveway. *Beck Handyman Service* was printed in red and blue letters.

"Looks like he's here," Jessie said.

"I want to ring the doorbell!" Benny shouted. He liked ringing doorbells.

"If you keep shouting like that," Violet said, smiling, "we won't have to ring the doorbell!"

Benny ran to the door and rang the doorbell. He rang it a second time. He was about to ring the bell a third time when Jessie ran and caught his hand and said, "Benny! That's enough!"

Mr. Beck opened the door and smiled at the children. "Look who's here! All four Alden children! What can I do for you?"

"We have a question," Henry said. "On Saturday when you were working at our house, you said you have to watch out with these old windows in the summer. What did you mean?"

"The windows in your house were getting tight and hard to open," he said. "Old windows are fragile and can break easily."

"What would you think if an air conditioner was running on a very hot day," Henry said, "so the air inside was very cold...could that make a window break?"

"Extreme temperature changes are very bad for old glass," Mr. Beck said. "Very cold inside, and very hot outside? Yes, that could cause a spontaneous break. Why?"

"Spontaneous!" Benny cried. "Like putting ice in hot coffee! The glass can break!"

"Exactly," said Mr. Beck.

"The air conditioning was running in the old Gerry's General Store building," Henry said. "The police think it was vandalism. People are blaming Kayla. But maybe the old window broke because of the cold inside and hot outside."

"I read about that broken window in the newspaper," Mr. Beck said. "The newspaper didn't say anything about an air conditioner running."

"The air conditioner was definitely running," Jessie said. "I'm surprised Mrs. Leob didn't mention that to the police. I wonder why it was on."

"That was an old building," said Mr. Beck. "The air conditioner was probably old, too. It probably just went haywire. Turned on by itself. The windows got icy cold, the sun beat down, and *wham*, the window broke."

"Perhaps we should tell the police," Violet said. "They might not know the inside was freezing and that extreme temperature changes can cause old glass to break."

"I will do that," Mr. Beck said. "I will head over there right away. They can investigate to see if that was what broke the window."

The children thanked Mr. Beck. They all said goodbye.

When the children were back on the sidewalk heading home, Jessie said, "It's nice

to know the broken window probably wasn't vandalism. The problem is, we're no closer to figuring out who wrote that letter and caused Kayla all these problems."

Violet said, "At least people will stop blaming Kayla for the broken window."

"I was really starting to think Ashley had broken the window," Jessie said. "She kept acting strangely about the golf ball."

"Maybe there is still a clue there," Henry said. "There was something strange about all those golf balls on the floor of the store. Why don't you just ask her what she knows about the golf ball? You're the team captain, after all. The ball was used to trip a team member. You have a good reason to ask her."

"All right, I'll ask her tomorrow," Jessie said. "Maybe there still is a connection between the golf balls and the letter writer, even though I can't imagine what the connection can possibly be."

***

That night, long after the rest of the family was asleep, Violet heard Jessie tossing in her bed.

"Are you awake?" Violet whispered.

"Yes," Jessie said. "I'm thinking about Kayla. Why are you awake?"

"I keep thinking about Kayla, too," Violet said.

The only light in the room came from a small night light in the bathroom just down the hallway. There was just enough light so Violet could see the outline of her stuffed animals on the shelf near her bed.

"I would love to be an international soccer mascot," Jessie whispered. "But not like this. Not because someone else is having bad fortune."

"I know what you mean," Violet whispered back.

"If we don't get to the bottom of this," Jessie said, "I'll have to say I don't want to go."

Just then, words popped into Violet's head: *Things aren't always as they seem.*

Violet's teacher had said that once. Violet agreed completely that things were not always as they seemed. For example, a lot of people

disliked Kayla. A lot of people were jealous of Kayla, too. So it seemed like someone who didn't like her and was jealous of her wrote the mean letter. *But maybe that wasn't what happened at all*, Violet realized.

She thought about the golf balls. Because golf balls were found inside Gerry's General Store, and because Kayla had a golf ball in her hand, so it seemed like there was a connection between Kayla and the broken window. But what if there was more to the story?

Violet knew that sometimes, with mysteries, the clue is where something doesn't quite feel right.

For Violet, the part that didn't feel right was Kayla's attitude toward soccer. She didn't seem to even like soccer. Who would have thought that?

Everyone criticized Kayla for not being a team player. But if she didn't even like soccer, no wonder she wasn't a good team player.

Violet put her head on the pillow and closed her eyes. Jessie's breathing was so deep and steady, Violet knew she had fallen

asleep. Violet still felt puzzled, but she felt comforted as always by the nearness of her sister. Soon she, too, fell asleep.

CHAPTER 9

A Confession

The next morning, at school, lots of Jessie's classmates came to congratulate her on being asked to be mascot.

Jessie said thank you, always adding, "But I don't think I'll go. I don't think it's fair to Kayla."

"I'm *sure* you'll go, Jessie," Danielle said coldly.

Jessie turned to look at Danielle, astonished.

"Everyone keeps thinking I wrote that letter," Danielle said, "because I don't like

Kayla. Here's what I wonder. I wonder if *Jessie* wrote the letter because she knew Coach Olson likes her best, so she knew she'd get to go to Brazil as mascot!"

"I did not write that letter," Jessie said, horrified.

Just then, Ashley walked over to join them. "Maybe it was Jessie who wrote the letter!" Ashley said.

Jessie folded her arms across her chest and looked at Ashley. "Tell me about that golf ball Danielle used to trip Kayla," Jessie said. "What do you know about it?"

As before, the mention of the golf ball had a strange effect on Ashley. She looked quickly away and didn't say anything. She rocked on the balls of her feet, as if she wanted to run away.

No doubt, there was something going on with Ashley and that golf ball.

"It's okay," Jessie said gently. "You can tell me. I don't think you broke the window. Something seems strange, though, about the whole thing. A bunch of golf balls were found

inside the store. Danielle used a golf ball to trip Kayla. Then people started blaming Kayla for breaking the window when I know she didn't."

Ashley had a pained, guilty look on her face. Jessie suspected Ashley was about to make a confession. She was thus surprised when Ashley cried, "I didn't break the window either! I promise."

"I know you didn't," Jessie said. "Mr. Beck, the handyman, knows about old windows. He said it probably broke by itself."

"Well, good, because I didn't break the window," Ashley said.

"Then why do you act strangely every time someone mentions the golf ball?" Jessie asked.

Ashley narrowed her eyes. A moment passed. Then another. Jessie thought Ashley was about to say something mean. Instead, she said, "I was walking to practice on Wednesday, and I went by the old store. The window was broken and inside were some golf balls. I reached in and picked one up. While we were waiting for practice, Danielle

and I were rolling it back and forth."

"I see," Jessie said. "The truth is that you stole the golf ball."

Ashley looked horrified. "It was just laying there! It didn't belong to anyone! The store was abandoned! It really wasn't stealing!"

Jessie didn't answer.

"It wasn't," Ashley said. Then she softened and looked genuinely frightened. "Was it?"

"It *was* stealing," Jessie said. "Why did you take it?"

"It was just sitting there inside the window. I don't know. I shouldn't have."

"Just go put it back," Jessie said.

"I would, but Kayla still has it. I can't ask her for it back. She'll wonder why I'm asking. Then she'll figure out I stole it, then she'll tell everyone I stole it to get back at me for being mean."

"Maybe she won't," Jessie said. Then she had an idea. "Do you want me to get it back from her?"

"Would you?" Ashley said. "Oh, thank you!"

***

Jessie was walking home from school when she was surprised by a tap on her shoulder.

She turned. There was Kayla, smiling. "Thanks," Kayla said.

Jessie knew right away Kayla was thanking her for standing up for her about the window.

"It was nothing," Jessie said. "I just knew you didn't break that window."

"It was awfully nice of you," Kayla said.

Then Jessie remembered Ashley and the golf ball. "Oh, by the way, do you still have that golf ball?"

"Yes," Kayla said. "Why?"

"I know who it belongs to. Will you give it to me so I can return it?"

"Sure!" Kayla waved, then walked off in the direction of her own house.

***

When Jessie arrived home, she immediately went to look for Henry. He was already in his bedroom, sitting at his desk, doing homework. When she entered his room, he set down his pencil and turned to her. She told him everything, including the mean

thing Danielle had suggested.

"Someone in my class said that, too," Henry said. "Someone who doesn't know you at all suggested you wrote the letter so you could be mascot."

Jessie sat down gloomily. "We have to figure out who wrote the letter!" she said.

Henry said, "Let's gather everyone together so we can go over our clues. It's snack time, anyway."

All four children sat together at the table in the kitchen eating their after-school snack. Mrs. McGregor had made banana bread, which they ate with milk. "This is the best banana bread Mrs. McGregor has ever made!" Benny said, as he helped himself to another slice.

The children went over all their clues. Given how many people disliked Kayla, they were surprised to realize they had only three real suspects: Mr. Olson, Danielle, and Ashley. Jessie added another name. "Mia said she thought I should be mascot, so she is a suspect, too."

"Who's Mia?" Benny asked.

"She's the high school girl who helps coaches my team," Jessie said.

The problem was Jessie was pretty sure neither Danielle or Ashley had written the letter. Nobody really believed Mr. Olson had done it. And there wasn't much to connect Mia to the letter, either.

The Alden children looked at each other in silence.

Suddenly Violet said, "There is one other suspect we haven't thought of who might have written that letter."

Everyone looked at her.

"Who?" Henry asked.

"Kayla," Violet said.

The children looked at her, stunned.

"She doesn't even like soccer," Violet said. "She told me. Her parents filled out the application. I think they push her to play soccer when she'd rather not. I think she'd rather draw."

"That explains why she hasn't acted upset about not being mascot," Jessie said.

"Do you think she sabotaged her own chances?" Henry asked. "Why not just say she didn't want to be mascot?"

"Maybe she thought the letter would be easier than telling her parents the truth," Violet said.

The children were quiet, considering this.

"Well," Jessie said. "Her mother is very forceful."

Henry said, "Kayla's new in town, so she might not know about the automatic save function at the library."

"Even if she knew," Jessie said, "why would she care? Nobody would suspect her. They'd think it was Danielle or someone else who is mean to her."

"If Kayla wrote the letter," Henry said, "she'll never tell anyone."

"She might tell me," Violet said.

"How are you going to get her to tell you?" Jessie asked.

"I don't know yet," Violet said.

***

Kayla was in the glade with her sketch pad

when Violet arrived. Violet smiled, sat down, and took out her pencils. To Violet's surprise, she also took out a golf ball.

"Can you give this to Jessie for me?"

"Certainly," Violet said. They drew for a long time in silence. At last, Violet put her pencil down and said, "There is something bad happening. It has to do with Jessie."

"Jessie?" Kayla looked instantly concerned.

"People are saying Jessie wrote that letter to the mascot committee because she wanted to be mascot. People say she knew she was Coach Olson's favorite and if your chances were ruined, she'd get to be mascot."

"Everyone should know Jessie would never do something like that," Kayla said.

Kayla frowned and went back to her sketch pad. The two girls drew for a while in silence. Violet was not concentrating on her drawing. She sensed that Kayla wasn't either.

Violet took a deep breath and said, "Do you know what I think?" Violet knew it was easier for shy people to listen to other people's ideas than to answer direct questions. So she said,

"I think you wrote the letter." She said this in a matter-of-fact way.

"Ridiculous," Kayla said. She went on drawing.

"I just thought maybe you wrote the letter because your parents are so serious about soccer."

"They are serious," Kayla said. "*Too* serious, if you ask me."

They drew in silence again. After a while, Kayla said, "Do people really think Jessie would write that letter?"

"It looks bad, doesn't it? Someone writes a letter, then Jessie gets to be mascot. You can see how people might think that."

Kayla sprang to her feet. "Well it's not true! Jessie did *not* write the letter." Kayla scooped up her pencils and sketchpad. "I have to go now," she said, and ran off through the woods.

Violet scooped up her own pencils and sketchpad and ran after her. Kayla was a good runner, much better than Violet. Violet had to run her fastest to keep up. When Kayla

turned right at the street, Violet understood Kayla was heading toward the soccer field.

***

Jessie had come early to soccer practice that day. Coach Olson, and a few of the girls, were already there. Mia had said she couldn't coach, so Coach Olson said he'd be there too so Henry wouldn't be on his own.

Jessie waved to Coach Olson. He waved back. She walked purposely toward him.

"Hey, Jessie, what's up?" he asked.

"I've been thinking," she said. "I believe someone is sabotaging Kayla. I just don't feel right accepting the invitation to be mascot because—"

They both looked up to see Mrs. Thompson marching across the street toward them.

"Oh, no," Coach Olson said. "It looks like something else has happened."

"Has anyone seen Kayla?" Mrs. Thompson asked loudly.

Coach Olson looked around. "She doesn't seem to be here yet."

"I haven't been able to find her all afternoon. Lately she's been disappearing for hours at a time."

"Here she comes now!" Jessie said, pointing.

Kayla jogged toward them. Tucked under her arm was a sketch pad. Her face was flushed from the heat, her neck and forehead wet with perspiration.

That was when Jessie noticed that Violet, too, was running from the same direction. Violet was panting. Jessie ran for her own

water bottle and gave it to Violet, who drank some, then splashed water on her face.

"Whew!" Violet said. "It's hot!"

"What's going on?" Jessie whispered.

"I'm not completely sure," Violet whispered back.

"Where have you been?" Mrs. Thompson asked Kayla.

"In the woods, drawing." Kayla's voice was low and remarkably steady for someone who had just sprinted in the heat.

"Why?" Mrs. Thompson asked.

Instead of answering the question, Kayla said, "I cannot have people saying that Jessie wrote that letter sabotaging me. Jessie is much too nice. She didn't do it."

"And how do you know that?" Mrs. Thompson said.

"Because *I* wrote the letter," Kayla said.

There was stunned silence. Then Mrs. Thompson said, "What?"

"I never thought it would blow up this way!" Kayla said. "I never thought there would be a big scandal. I thought you'd keep it all

hush-hush. I thought you'd be embarrassed. I didn't think you'd march onto the soccer field and tell the whole town about it!"

Mrs. Thompson stared, astonished. She opened her mouth to speak, but then closed her mouth. There was a long silence. Jessie found herself smiling. She supposed Mrs. Thompson wasn't often at a loss for words.

At last, Mrs. Thompson asked, "Why on earth would you do such a thing?"

Kayla didn't answer.

Violet leaned and whispered to Jessie, "She wrote the letter because she didn't want to play soccer anymore."

Jessie stepped forward and, to Mrs. Thompson, said, "Ma'am, maybe Kayla wrote the letter because she didn't want to play soccer any more. Maybe she didn't want to be a mascot."

"Oh, don't be silly," Mrs. Thompson snapped.

"Well, I didn't!" Kayla said. "It was too much! Soccer, soccer, soccer. All the time. Every day. Nothing else but soccer! I told

you I wanted to do the drawing class and you said, 'but what about soccer.'"

Violet squeezed Jessie's hand.

Things are not what they seem.

Kayla wasn't a snooty show-off, like everyone thought. She was unhappy. She was shy and quiet. She wanted to be left in peace, with her sketch pad. She acted badly because she didn't want to play any more.

Kayla turned to Jessie. "I hope you decide to accept the invitation. You deserve it. You'd be a wonderful mascot."

CHAPTER 10

Prime Time Soccer

Thousands of people cheered and waved flags and banners. The stadium was so crowded, the Aldens held on to each other as they made their way to their seats. All around people were speaking different languages.

"I can't believe we are in Rio de Janeiro!" Henry said.

"I'll bet there are one million people in this stadium!" Benny said.

"Almost," Henry said. "This stadium holds almost seventy-five thousand people."

"Seventy-five thousand!" Benny repeated, astonished. "How many zeroes is that?"

"Three," said Henry.

Up ahead, a child accidentally dropped the churro he was eating. Benny watched the churro drop and said, "Poor Watch. He'd love to be here!"

"He could make all the noise he wanted," Violet said. "And nobody would even hear."

"And he could eat the food people are dropping," Benny said.

Benny liked the smells of all the different foods. Most of the food for sale in the booths he didn't recognize, but they all smelled delicious. He looked forward to lunch! No boring hot dogs and peanuts for him! He was looking forward to trying new Brazilian food.

Aloud he said, "This is much better than a coupon for a free cone at Igloo Ice Cream! A million times better!"

Grandfather, Henry, Violet, and Benny sat in the special seats reserved for family members of mascots.

"The opening ceremony will start soon," Henry said, checking his watch.

"Yay!" Benny shouted.

Violet smiled. She was happy things worked out so well. Somewhere in these thousands of people, Kayla was here with her parents. Kayla's parents still wanted to come to the tournament. Kayla was happy to go, as long as she didn't have to walk onto the field in front of millions of people and as long as she didn't have to play soccer if she didn't want to. The Thompsons were staying at the same hotel as the Aldens. That morning, they'd all had breakfast together.

Kayla's parents let her sign up for the Monday after school art class. Kayla was multi-talented. She was a good artist and a good soccer player. She also knew how to be a good friend.

Ashley's attitude toward Kayla changed as well. After Jessie gave her the golf ball, and Ashley returned it to the store, Ashley stopped being mean to Kayla. In fact, the next time Danielle started saying something

unkind to Kayla, Ashley stopped her.

The marching band came onto the field, but the crowd was cheering so loudly the children could only hear the beating of the drums. Then came the spectacular fireworks.

"Look at that one over there!" Benny shouted, pointing to the sky. "Fireworks!"

"I like that one!" Violet shouted, pointing. "Lavender fireworks! Amazing!"

A singer stood on the stage and sang. The crowd quieted so the children could hear her singing. Her voice was smooth and rich. Violet could not understand the words, but the music was breathtakingly beautiful.

Next, two expert soccer players did a demonstration. They dribbled the ball up and down the field, showing the most amazing footwork—kicking the ball in surprising directions, kicking it into the air and bouncing it up and down on their heads and shoulders, keeping it moving in the air without ever using their hands.

"They're so good," Violet said, "they make Kayla look like a beginner!"

"I wish I could do that!" Benny said.

"Maybe you can," Grandfather suggested. "If you practice enough."

"I am going to practice as soon as we get home!" Benny said. "I am going to practice and practice! Maybe one day I will be in a real tournament!"

At last, it was time for the child mascots to walk onto the field with the players. The Aldens watched excitedly for Jessie.

"There she is!" Benny shouted. "I see her!"

Indeed, Jessie was just then walking on the field alongside one of the team members. The spectators cheered and stamped their feet. People waved streamers. Jessie turned and waved.

Henry, Benny, and even Violet clapped loudly, stamped their feet, and shouted, "Yay, Jessie! Yay, Jessie!"

Benny bounded out of his seat, pointed to the field, and shouted at the top of his voice, "That's my sister over there." He jumped up and down a few times. "That's my sister over there!"

Jessie had, by now, walked all the way around the field. Just before she stepped out of the spotlight, she turned once more and waved to her family.

Grandfather smiled. "I am so proud of her. I am proud of all of you."

THE BOXCAR
CHILDREN BEGINNING

by Patricia MacLachlan

*Before they were the Boxcar Children, Henry,
Jessie, Violet, and Benny Alden lived with
their parents on Fair Meadow Farm.*

978-0-8075-6617-6
US $5.99 paperback

Although times are hard, they're happy—"the best family of all,"
Mama likes to say. And when a traveling family needs shelter
from a winter storm, the Aldens help, and make new friends. But
the spring and summer bring events that will change all their
lives forever.

Newbery Award-winning author Patricia MacLachlan tells a
wonderfully moving story of the Alden children's origins.

* * *

"Fans will enjoy this picture of life 'before.'"—*Publishers Weekly*

"An approachable lead-in that serves to fill in the background
both for confirmed fans and readers new to the series."
—*Kirkus Reviews*

THE BOXCAR CHILDREN SPOOKTACULAR SPECIAL

created by Gertrude Chandler Warner

Three spooky stories in one big book!

From ghosts to zombies to a haunting in their very own backyard, the Boxcar Children have plenty of spooktacular adventures in these three exciting mysteries.

978-0-8075-7605-2
US $9.99 paperback

THE ZOMBIE PROJECT
The story about the Winding River zombie is just an old legend. But Benny sees a strange figure lurching through the woods and thinks the zombie could be real!

THE MYSTERY OF THE HAUNTED BOXCAR
One night the Aldens see a mysterious light shining inside the boxcar where they once lived. Soon they discover spooky new clues to the old train car's past!

THE PUMPKIN HEAD MYSTERY
Every year the Aldens help out with the fun at a pumpkin farm. Can they find out why a ghost with a jack-o'-lantern head is haunting the hayrides?

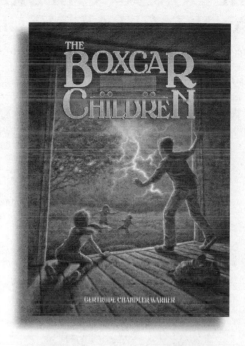

#1 THE BOXCAR CHILDREN
THE BOXCAR CHILDREN® MYSTERIES
HC 978-0-8075-0851-0
$15.99/$17.99 Canada
PB 978-0-8075-0852-7
$5.99/$6.99 Canada
*"One warm night four children stood in front
of a bakery. No one knew them. No one knew
where they had come from."* So begins Gertrude
Chandler Warner's beloved story about four
orphans who run away and find shelter in an
abandoned boxcar. There they manage to live all
on their own, and at last, find love and security
from an unexpected source.

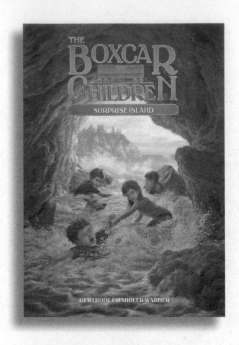

#2 SURPRISE ISLAND
THE BOXCAR CHILDREN® MYSTERIES
HC 978-0-8075-7673-1
$15.99/$17.99 Canada
PB 978-0-8075-7674-8
$5.99/$6.99 Canada
The Boxcar Children have a home with their
grandfather now—but their adventures are just
beginning! Their first adventure is to spend the
summer camping on their own private island.
The island is full of surprises, including a kind
stranger with a secret.

#3 THE YELLOW HOUSE MYSTERY
THE BOXCAR CHILDREN® MYSTERIES
HC 978-0-8075-9365-3
$15.99/$17.99 Canada
PB 978-0-8075-9366-0
$5.99/$6.99 Canada
Henry, Jessie, Violet, and Benny Alden discover
that a mystery surrounds the rundown yellow
house on Surprise Island. The children find a
letter and other clues that lead them to the trail
of a man who vanished from the house.

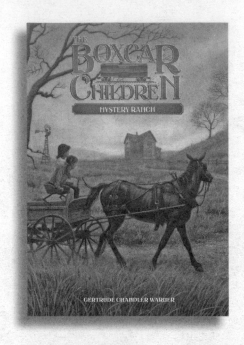

#4 MYSTERY RANCH
THE BOXCAR CHILDREN® MYSTERIES
HC 978-0-8075-5390-9
$15.99/$17.99 Canada
PB 978-0-8075-5391-6
$5.99/$6.99 Canada
Henry, Jessie, Violet, and Benny Alden just
found out they have an Aunt Jane and travel out
west to spend the summer on her ranch. While
there, they make an amazing discovery about
the ranch that will change Aunt Jane's life.

GERTRUDE CHANDLER WARNER discovered when she was teaching that many readers who like an exciting story could find no books that were both easy and fun to read. She decided to try to meet this need, and her first book, *The Boxcar Children*, quickly proved she had succeeded.

Miss Warner drew on her own experiences to write the mystery. As a child she spent hours watching trains go by on the tracks opposite her family home. She often dreamed about what it would be like to set up housekeeping in a caboose or freight car—the situation the Alden children find themselves in.

While the mystery element is central to each of Miss Warner's books, she never thought of them as strictly juvenile mysteries. She liked to stress the Aldens' independence and resourcefulness and their solid New England devotion to using up and making do. The Aldens go about most of their adventures with as little adult supervision as possible—something else that delights young readers.

Miss Warner lived in Putnam, Connecticut, until her death in 1979. During her lifetime, she received hundreds of letters from girls and boys telling her how much they liked her books.

DISCARD

The Boxcar Children Mysteries

The Boxcar Children
Surprise Island
The Yellow House Mystery
Mystery Ranch
Mike's Mystery
Blue Bay Mystery
The Woodshed Mystery
The Lighthouse Mystery
Mountain Top Mystery
Schoolhouse Mystery
Caboose Mystery
Houseboat Mystery
Snowbound Mystery
Tree House Mystery
Bicycle Mystery
Mystery in the Sand
Mystery Behind the Wall
Bus Station Mystery
Benny Uncovers a Mystery
The Haunted Cabin Mystery
The Deserted Library Mystery
The Animal Shelter Mystery
The Old Motel Mystery
The Mystery of the Hidden Painting
The Amusement Park Mystery
The Mystery of the Mixed-Up Zoo
The Camp-Out Mystery
The Mystery Girl
The Mystery Cruise
The Disappearing Friend Mystery
The Mystery of the Singing Ghost
The Mystery in the Snow
The Pizza Mystery
The Mystery Horse
The Mystery at the Dog Show
The Castle Mystery
The Mystery of the Lost Village
The Mystery on the Ice
The Mystery of the Purple Pool
The Ghost Ship Mystery
The Mystery in Washington, DC

The Canoe Trip Mystery
The Mystery of the Hidden Beach
The Mystery of the Missing Cat
The Mystery at Snowflake Inn
The Mystery on Stage
The Dinosaur Mystery
The Mystery of the Stolen Music
The Mystery at the Ball Park
The Chocolate Sundae Mystery
The Mystery of the Hot Air Balloon
The Mystery Bookstore
The Pilgrim Village Mystery
The Mystery of the Stolen Boxcar
The Mystery in the Cave
The Mystery on the Train
The Mystery at the Fair
The Mystery of the Lost Mine
The Guide Dog Mystery
The Hurricane Mystery
The Pet Shop Mystery
The Mystery of the Secret Message
The Firehouse Mystery
The Mystery in San Francisco
The Niagara Falls Mystery
The Mystery at the Alamo
The Outer Space Mystery
The Soccer Mystery
The Mystery in the Old Attic
The Growling Bear Mystery
The Mystery of the Lake Monster
The Mystery at Peacock Hall
The Windy City Mystery
The Black Pearl Mystery
The Cereal Box Mystery
The Panther Mystery
The Mystery of the Queen's Jewels
The Stolen Sword Mystery
The Basketball Mystery
The Movie Star Mystery
The Mystery of the Pirate's Map
The Ghost Town Mystery